# Screech Team

## The Bigfoot in the End Zone

**by Bill Doyle**

**Illustrated by Jared Lee**

Scholastic Inc.

For the Hunter clan
—B.D.

To Mary Jo Day
—J.L.

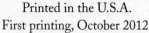

ISBN 978-0-545-47977-6

12 11 10 9 8 7 6 5 4 3 2 1     12 13 14 15 16 17/0

Printed in the U.S.A.          40
First printing, October 2012

Book design by Jennifer Rinaldi Windau

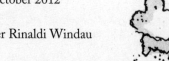

# CHAPTER 1
## Monster Blitz

Three monsters snarled as they rushed at Karl.

He stumbled a few steps back and almost tripped. *Stay calm!* he told himself.

The charging creatures were just inches away. Karl had to act. It was now or never. He cocked his arm and threw the football—

*Ka-klam!*

The monsters crashed into Karl and lifted the werewolf off the ground. Sailing through the air, Karl kept one eye on the ball as it wobbled toward the end zone.

*Floosh!* Karl splashed into a pool of mud under the three tacklers. He spit out a lump of warm sludge and laughed. "You guys are the best!"

His best friend, J.D. the ghost, floated over his head. Eric the blob was squished under his chin. And Dennis the vampire had a fang jammed up Karl's nose.

With the start of football season still a week away, tonight the Scream Team was playing a 5-on-4 scrimmage against themselves. Their coaches hadn't arrived yet, so they were just messing around on the muddy gridiron.

Karl couldn't wait for the real games to start. More than anything he wanted to play in the midseason Wolfenstein Muck Bowl.

You needed to be invited to play in the Muck Bowl. The Frankensteins always got chosen because they were so popular. The other spot was completely up for grabs. If the Scream Team won their first three games, they'd have a better chance at it. And

Karl might finally meet his hero, Wolfenstein! Every year, the Monster League legend and repeat all-star took part in the Muck Bowl halftime show.

Now, Karl hopped to his feet so he could see down the football field. Patsy the zombie had just missed the pass, and the play was over.

But Bolt the Frankenstein's monster was still steaming straight toward Patsy. One of his legs had belonged to a ballet dancer who was always looking for a bathroom. So it never wanted to stop moving.

"Bolt leg stop now!" Bolt yelled at his leg. No good.

He barreled into Patsy. Her body parts exploded everywhere.

"Late hit!" Patsy shouted. Then she burst out laughing and put herself back together.

"My side's turn for the ball," J.D. said. "Come on, Karl!"

Karl's tail wagged. There was only one thing the werewolf loved more than playing quarterback for one side. It was playing quarterback for both! Since it was just a scrimmage, no one cared if Karl played QB the entire game.

The two sides lined up and waited for the kickoff. The Scream Team didn't have a football holder or any other equipment yet. So Beck the bigfoot waddled over to a mushroom mouth that was sprouting on the field. He stuck one end of the ball into the biting plant.

Then Beck took a few steps back. Karl watched his friend, knowing what would come next.

A goofy smile lit up Beck's face and his eyes got all sparkly. He always looked like this when he was about to kick the football.

"This is the best part of the game!" Beck yelled. His feet were at least three times the size of any other bigfoot. Whenever he kicked the ball, it was like a hammer whacking a pebble. He pulled back one giant foot and—

"Nice flippers! You going scuba diving?" someone shouted from the sidelines. "Hee hoo hee!"

*Pffft*. You could almost hear the cruel laugh sucking all the fun off the field.

It hit Beck like a bucket of cold slime, and he froze with his foot in the air. Beck's furry face turned red. Karl looked over to the sidelines to see who was teasing him.

No surprise.

Dr. Neuron, the president of the Junior Club Monster League, stood there.

"Ahh!" Dennis shrieked. His bat wings popped out on his back and started flitting in panic. Karl couldn't blame him. Dr. Neuron was always out to destroy the Scream Team.

"Here we go again," J.D. groaned. "He tried to trash our baseball and basketball seasons. What's he going to take away from us now?"

Dr. Neuron held up a few tentacles as he walked toward them. "No, no," he said. "I'm not here to *take* anything. I'm actually here to *give* you something."

"What?" Patsy asked. "A case of the molten mumps?"

Dr. Neuron's eyes bugged out. "Oh," he said with a fake chuckle. "I forgot how incredibly charming you monsters are. No, here's my gift."

With that, Dr. Neuron stepped aside. A smaller monster had been hiding behind him the whole time. It was a mini version of Dr. Neuron, right down to the tentacles.

"This is Happy, my nephew," Dr. Neuron explained. "For some very strange reason he doesn't want to play sports. All he likes is to put on crunch bug puppet shows." As he said *puppet shows*, he gagged like he might throw up. "My sister has been nagging me to put him in the JCML. I want Happy to join your team."

Happy kept his head down so the Scream Team couldn't really see his face. But Karl could tell he was smiling.

"Don't forget, you're the Scream Team, who accepts *anyone*," Dr. Neuron said.

*Good point*, Karl thought.

When Karl and his friends had first formed the Scream Team, no one else had wanted them. Not the Werewolves, Blobs, Ghosts . . . no one. Now they were the only team in the league made up of different kinds of monsters.

"Besides, you need ten players on the field to play JCML football. Right now you only have nine. Are you going to tell my poor nephew he's not wanted?" Dr. Neuron asked.

"Our coaches aren't here yet," Karl said, trying to stall so he could think things over.

"Then the decision is up to you and your teammates," Dr. Neuron said. "I would consider it a personal favor to me. One that could be rewarded."

"How?" Patsy asked.

Dr. Neuron thought for a second, then said, "As long as your ragtag team can manage not to lose all of your games, I think we can arrange an

invitation to be one of the teams in the Muck Bowl this year. . . ."

The Muck Bowl! Karl would do anything to get his team there. Plus, he knew what it was like to have hurt feelings. He didn't want to make anyone feel that way. "Huddle up, Scream Team," he said, and gathered with his friends a few feet from the Neurons. "What do you guys think?" he asked.

"Dr. Neuron is right," J.D. said. "We *do* need another monster to have ten players."

Maxwell shrugged. "And his name *is* Happy."

"We'll need all the help we can get to beat the Frankensteins . . . in the MUCK BOWL!" Karl exclaimed.

Everyone nodded and the huddle broke apart. "Okay, Dr. Neuron," Karl said. "Happy can be on the team, and—"

But Dr. Neuron wasn't listening. Having heard *okay*, he was already rushing off the field, back to his limo.

Happy lifted his head all the way. Now the

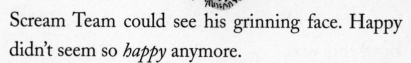

Scream Team could see his grinning face. Happy didn't seem so *happy* anymore.

"He looks more like his name should be Wicked, or Nasty," Mike said, loud enough for Happy to hear.

But instead of being angry, Happy just laughed. "Hee hoo hee!"

Karl's ears perked straight up, realizing they had just made a monstrous mistake. "You're the one who laughed at Beck!"

"Abso-tootly," Happy said, snatching the football out of Karl's paws. "I'm also the one who's going to play quarterback for the Scream Team."

# CHAPTER 2
## Quarterback Sneak

Karl thought he must be hearing things. He jammed his paws in his ears to clear out any clumps of earwax.

"Um, you can't play quarterback, Happy," he said. "That position is already taken. By me."

Happy's creepy grin doubled in size. "I'm not going to argue with a shaved cat."

"I'm not a cat!" Karl said. "I'm a werewolf."

Karl knew his coat *was* a little patchy. He'd been called a poodle—even a spotted miniature pony—

but never a shaved cat.

"Really?" Happy acted puzzled. He looked at the rest of the Scream Team. "He's not a cat?"

Karl growled.

Just then, a van swerved into the nearby parking lot. It jerked side to side as if the steering wheel was being tugged back and forth. The van screeched to a halt.

Dennis sighed in relief. "The Coaches Conundrum are here. They'll sort this out."

"You think?" Patsy asked doubtfully.

Coach Wyatt and his brother, Virgil, were part of a two-headed monster. They had different heads and shared the same body. But that was all they had in common. They had different ideas about everything, and the team could hear them bickering as they crossed the field.

"Who's this?" Wyatt asked gruffly, pointing at Happy. "He looks like a spy to me."

Karl realized a lie would solve his new problem. He could say Happy was a spy. Coach Wyatt was

so freaked out about spies that there was no way he would let Happy play quarterback.

"This is Happy. He wants to join the team," Karl said, sticking with the truth. He figured that might be worse anyway. "He's Dr. Neuron's nephew."

"Well, you can't help who you're related to," Virgil chirped. "I should know."

Wyatt frowned at his brother. "Are you still telling people we're related?" he snapped. "There's no proof of that. Besides, I'll decide who's on the team. After all, I'm the offensive coach."

"Got that right, dude." Virgil held his nose and made a comical face. "You are pretty offensive."

"Well," Wyatt said, "at least I don't think de*fense* is something that goes around a farm. Some defensive coach you are!"

Happy did a little dance as if he loved fighting. "Hee hoo hee!" he laughed. "So it's decided. I'll play quarterback."

Karl started to say something. But Coach Virgil beat him to the punch. "Happy, dude—chill," he said. "Today we'll run through drills to figure out who will play what. We'll match your aura to the position of your destiny."

"Oh brother," Wyatt said, rolling his eyes. "Whoever wants to be quarterback, follow me. The rest of you go with Virgil to work on blocking."

With both brothers pulling in different directions, no one went anywhere. Finally, Karl and Happy walked over to stand next to Wyatt's half of the coaches' body, and the rest of the team grouped together on Virgil's half.

"Quarterbacks need to think fast under pressure," Coach Wyatt said to Happy and Karl. "See that giant pile of fish heads next to the trash bin? Three weeks ago, I hid a bologna sandwich from my brother in there. The first one of you to find the sandwich wins a point!"

Karl hesitated. "What does this have to do with football?"

Coach Wyatt shrugged. "I'm hungry."

Happy wasn't waiting. By the time Karl jumped into the pile, Happy was digging through the fish heads with his tentacles. He found the sandwich in a flash.

"That's one point for Happy," Coach Wyatt said. The next drill was called Spinpuke. Happy and Karl were supposed to run around in circles for a couple of minutes and then sprint in a straight line. But Karl didn't stop spinning. He spotted something just at the edge of his vision and tried to catch it.

"Get it, Karl!" Happy shouted from down the field. He was already done with the drill.

His laugh made Karl realize something was wrong. Karl was actually chasing his tail. Something he did when he got nervous.

"That's another point for Happy," Coach Wyatt said. "One last drill, quarterback wannabes. Throw this ripe pus bag twenty yards without letting it pop."

Karl carefully lifted a jiggly pus bag and threw it. His wobbly pass hit the ground and exploded everywhere. Karl groaned, but Mike the swamp thing started rolling around in the slime. "Nothing like a pus bath!" he said cheerfully.

When it was Happy's turn, he sucked the pus out of the bag and held it in his mouth. He threw the empty bag twenty yards down the field. He walked to the bag, picked it up, squirted the pus back into it, and then sealed the bag shut.

"That was sneaky!" Karl said. But he had to admit it was also pretty clever. Karl had choked under pressure, and didn't have a single point.

He turned to Coach Wyatt. "I'm not going to get to be QB, am I?"

Coach Wyatt shrugged again. "Before we announce who is playing what, we still have to hold tryouts for kicker."

Beck was the only monster who wanted to be kicker. "I'll give it a shot," he said. He didn't sound as sure of himself anymore.

His flipper-sized feet flapped out onto the field. The coaches held the ball in place. Just as Beck was about to kick it, Happy laughed. "I've heard of a bigfoot," he crowed, "but I've never seen the BIGGEST foot!"

Beck stopped. He took a breath and then started toward the ball again.

"When you buy shoes do they charge you by the mile?" Happy tittered. Beck froze and lowered his kicking foot.

Before anyone else could speak, Happy fired off two more insults. "Too bad we're not on the slopes, you already have two huge skis! Is it hard to clip your toenails when they're in another time zone?"

"Enough!" Coach Wyatt shouted. Happy giggled one last time and finally closed his mouth.

By now, Beck's face had turned bright red. "I guess I don't want to be kicker anyway," he mumbled. He backed away from the ball and tried to hide in the middle of the team.

"That's all right, dude," Coach Virgil said to Beck. "We'll figure out who will be kicker later."

When the coaches wandered off to fight over who would play what position, Karl stomped over to Happy.

"Leave Beck alone," Karl snarled. "Nobody thinks what you're doing is funny."

"I do," Happy replied, pretending his feelings were hurt. "Are you saying I'm nobody, Karl? That's just mean of you."

Karl was so mad, he could only sputter. The

coaches walked over to the goalpost and taped up the list of players. They stood in front of the list, blocking everyone's view.

"We need a quarterback who can lead the team," Coach Wyatt said, looking directly at Happy. "Not one who makes fun of his teammates."

The coaches finally stepped aside so Karl and the rest of the team could read the list.

OFFENSE
Patsy—Wide receiver
Bolt—Guard
Eric—Wide receiver
Maxwell—Tackle
Dennis—Fullback
Beck—Running back
Mike—Guard
J.D.—Tackle
Happy—Center
Karl—Quarterback

Karl was QB! He pumped his paw in the air. "Yes!" He spotted Happy glaring at him but still smiling. "Sorry," Karl said.

"Oh, you will be," Happy said.

"What's that mean?" J.D. asked.

"I'd rather be home putting on crunch bug puppet shows than playing football," Happy explained. "My mom and my uncle are making me be here. The only spot I would have wanted is quarterback. And if I can't be QB . . ."

"What?" Karl asked.

Happy laughed wickedly and then answered, "I'm going to . . . tear the . . . Scream Team . . . APART."

# CHAPTER 3
## What a Pit!

Normally, Karl loved the stench of a football game. The smelly cups of old hot-dog water and the whiff of a hundred or so monsters sitting in the stands. But tonight when Karl walked into the stadium, he'd been too worried to enjoy any of it.

The start of the Scream Team's first game against the Bigfoots was just ten minutes away. And Happy couldn't be found anywhere. Their newest teammate hadn't bothered to show up to practice that week. So Karl and Happy were never able to work on their snaps.

"Over here, Karl!" Coach Virgil called, waving him over to the Scream Team bench. Their sponsor, Mr. Benedict, had brought crates filled with their game equipment. The mole man handed each monster a helmet, mouth guard, and shoulder pads.

The mouth guard covered only one of Dennis's fangs, and the shoulder pads weren't the best fit on Eric the blob.

"Who cares how we look?" Patsy said. "Without Happy we don't have enough players for the game anyway."

"Oh, Happy will be here," Mr. Benedict said. "He told me last night when he called to—"

"Hee hoo hee!" Happy's high-pitched laugh interrupted him. In the parking lot, Dr. Neuron was practically pushing Happy out of his limo.

"You will play football and you'll like it!" Dr. Neuron said before slamming the car door and speeding away.

Karl trotted over to Happy. "Hey, glad you're here," Karl said. When Happy didn't respond, he added, "Um, you didn't really mean what you said about wanting to tear the Scream Team apart, right?"

Happy grinned at him. "I'd be lying if I said I was telling the truth that that was a lie."

Karl scratched his head. "Oh, good, I guess," he said, confused. "Because if we win this game, we're one step closer to playing in the Wolfenstein Muck Bowl."

"I'm abso-tootly aware of that, my shaved-cat friend," Happy said, smiling. "It's all part of my plan."

Before Karl could ask what he meant, Hairy Hairwell's voice boomed from the loudspeakers. "Welcome, fiends and ghouls, to the first football

game of the JCML season!" the announcer shouted from his booth high above the stands. "Let's hear it for our referee of the evening, Frank the Cyclops!"

Frank waved to the crowd and performed the opening coin toss. "It's your call, Scream Team," the ref said. "What will it be? Do you want to kick or receive?"

Because they hadn't picked a kicker to replace Beck yet, Karl chose to receive.

"Big mistake," Happy said as the Scream Team lined up on one end of the field. In a flash, Karl knew he was right.

He should have realized that the Bigfoots would be good at anything that had to do with their feet . . . like kicking! Too late now. Frank blew the whistle. And the game started!

*Kablam!*

Micayla the Bigfoot kicked off just right. The football hurtled toward the end zone like a cannon shot and bounced out-of-bounds—touchback. The Scream Team had the ball at their own 20.

Karl called the first huddle of the game. His heart was pounding. The monsters on his team were all staring at him, waiting for him to be a leader. Happy just giggled.

Panicked, Karl glanced to the sidelines, hoping for help from the Coaches Conundrum. They were too busy drawing X's and O's in the dirt and fighting over which was more important, offensive or defensive plays.

"How about a scream pass?" Patsy suggested.

"Good idea," Karl said. "On *two*."

Beck stayed in the backfield with Karl, while the rest of the Scream Team went to the line. Karl stood behind Happy, who was center, and held out his paws for the snap.

When he saw that everyone was ready, Karl said, "Set . . . hut one . . . hut two!"

Karl waited for the snap . . . but nothing happened. Happy didn't move.

"Hut two!" Karl repeated. Still nothing. Then he started saying it over and over again. "Two, two, two!"

Frank finally blew the whistle. "Delay of game!" he shouted. "Five yard penalty. Offense."

"Why didn't you hike the ball when I said two, Happy?" Karl demanded once they were back in the huddle.

"Oh!" Happy giggled. "I thought you meant snap the ball on *too*. But you were saying *two*." Happy held out the ball. "Here, do you want it now?"

"No!" Karl shouted. "That play is over. For the next one, let's run razzle dazzle on *two*."

When they were lined up, Karl barked, "Hut one, hut two!" Happy wouldn't hike the ball, so Karl kept going. "Hut three, hut four, hut five!" He was on "hut twenty!" when Frank the ref blew the whistle and called another delay of game. This penalty pushed them back another five yards to their own 10-yard line.

The next play was the same story. Karl put out his paw for the snap.

"I'm waiting for the magic word," Happy said in a singsong voice.

"Hut two, *please*," Karl growled.

"Hmmm. No, that's not it."

"Abracadabra?"

"Try saying it on one foot," Happy suggested.

After the ref blew the whistle and called another penalty, the Scream Team was back in the huddle and it was fourth and 30 from their own goal line. They needed to punt.

"Beck, your feet are three times bigger than any other bigfoot," Karl said. "That means you could be three times better at kicking and punting. We need you!"

Beck seemed unsure but started walking to the backfield. With each step he took, Happy made a rude *flip-flap* sound as if Beck's feet were giant noisemakers.

Beck was too embarrassed to punt now. He shook his head. "Sorry, team. I can't do it."

"Okay," Karl said. He didn't want Beck to feel any worse. "We'll just try to run the ball."

The Scream Team went to the line. This time

when Karl said, "Hut two!" Happy just stood straight up. "Here you go," he said, and held out the football to the defensive tackle, Josh the Bigfoot.

Josh was so surprised, he hesitated. J.D. spotted what was happening and knocked it away. The ball spun through the air and landed in the hands of Maxwell the mummy.

"Who is that?" Maxwell said in surprise, feeling the weight in his hands. His wrapping had slid over his eyes and he couldn't see. "Eric, is that you?"

"Ish the foosball!" Dennis shouted, drool flying everywhere. "Runsh!"

"This way!" Mike called. He used his tail to pull on the end of Maxwell's wrapping. Like a yo-yo on a string, Maxwell swung around.

Now Maxwell was running in the right direction!
The closest Bigfoots were too far away to stop him.

"What a surprise turn of events!" Hairy Hairwell
shouted. "Maxwell the mummy of the Scream Team
can move! He's on the 45, the 40, the 35, the 30—"

*Phfft!*

Maxwell vanished. He was just gone.

# CHAPTER 4
## Abso-toot Chaos

"Where did Maxwell go?" Karl yelled.

Still running down the field, Mike started to say, "I don't—" *Phfft!* He dropped out of sight.

Beck rushed toward the end zone. "What's happen—" And he was gone as well.

Karl sprinted toward the sidelines, and *phfft!*

The last thing he heard was the crowd gasp as he disappeared from the field, too.

Karl fell through a hole in the field. He hit the muddy bottom six feet down.

He was just getting to his feet when Mr. Benedict popped up through the bottom of the hole. "Hello, Karl," the mole man said.

"What are you doing down here, Mr. Benedict?" Karl asked.

Mr. Benedict smiled. "I'm helping the referee dig tunnels underground so he can watch the game more closely."

"How could the referee watch the game from underground?" Karl asked, shaking his head. "And who told you that's what Frank the ref wanted?"

"Happy did," Mr. Benedict said. "When he called me yesterday."

Karl should have known! Happy had tricked Mr. Benedict! The mole man had created deep trenches and pits everywhere under the field.

As they crawled out of the hole together, Frank the referee was waiting on the surface. He threw flag after flag . . . after flag and started listing all the penalties while workers refilled the holes. "Delay of game. Extra player. Illegal burrowing. Offense. The Bigfoots will take possession of the ball."

Luckily, the Bigfoot team couldn't pass very far and they stumbled over each other's feet whenever they ran the ball. Still, they managed to reach the 40-yard line. From there, the Bigfoots easily scored a field goal.

Karl shouted to Coach Wyatt and Coach Virgil. "You have to take Happy out of the game! He's gone completely batty!"

"Heysh!" Dennis drooled. "Not cool!"

"We can't!" Wyatt called back. "We need ten players on the field!"

The Conundrums put Patsy at center and Happy at wide receiver. But it didn't matter what position he was playing. Happy kept finding ways of ruining things for the Scream Team. Happy tripped his own teammates and kept tackling Karl.

And he didn't even bother trying to hide what he was doing. "Hee hoo hee!" Happy laughed proudly again and again.

Before Karl knew it, the referee fired the game cannon.

"And that's the end of the game!" Hairy bellowed. "The Scream Team loses by 21 points on seven field goals from the Bigfoots."

The teams trotted through the line and shook hands. All except for Happy. He was still laughing too hard. The rest of the Scream Team clumped together and watched him roll on the ground giggling.

"He's going to do this every game," J.D. said. "We'll never win!"

Karl shook his head. If they kept losing they might not be invited to the Wolfenstein Muck Bowl. "Enough is enough," he growled. "I'm going to do something to stop Happy."

"What?" Mike asked.

Slapping his paws together, Karl answered, "Something drastic!"

# CHAPTER 5
## Burp Dreams

"You're throwing a party for Happy?" Patsy asked. "This is your drastic plan, Karl?"

Two nights after their first game, the Scream Team was packed inside Karl's tree fort in his backyard. They were waiting for Happy to arrive.

"A party seems like a good way to smooth things over with Happy," Karl said. "You know, because we got off on the wrong foot."

Beck was admiring Karl's Wolfenstein "Wolfie of the Year" poster. His head snapped around. "Wrong

foot? Who has the wrong foot?"

"Sorry, Beck, that's not what I meant." Karl changed the subject. "Let's try to have a good time."

Maxwell took a seat near the fort's hatchway. "Ah, this chair is comfy," he said.

"Umpph," the chair said.

Karl didn't have a talking chair. He looked more closely. Tentacles were waving underneath Maxwell. Happy must have popped up through the hatchway without anyone noticing. Karl rushed over to push Maxwell off of him.

"Sorry about that!" Karl said. "Welcome to the party, Happy! We can't wait to get to know you better."

Brushing himself off, Happy looked around, grinning. "What's to know?" Happy said with a shrug. "My name's Happy, I want to be a crunch bug puppeteer, and I'm going to destroy the Scream Team. If I manage to put up with you losers for the whole season, my uncle will buy me a puppet show."

"Oh, right," Karl said, trying to keep his temper. "Well, maybe you could get to know *us*. I like to collect sports stuff."

Happy just yawned. "Boring! I'm out of here. I've got to get home and work on evil plots to ruin the Scream Team."

"No!" Karl said. "Don't go yet!" He took a key from the chain around his neck and unlocked the wooden coffin-shaped case in the corner. Inside were five different glass jars, resting on a bed of straw.

"I never even look at these things unless I'm alone," Karl said. He pointed at one of the jars. "This one has a Wolfenstein sneeze complete with boogers."

Karl touched another jar. "This one has the chunky foot fungus scraped from Wolfenstein's socks."

"How'd you keep mini mouth biters from eating that?" Happy asked. "They can smell chunky foot fungus from miles away."

*Finally!* Karl thought. Something that interested Happy!

"The jar is airtight," Karl said. "So the mini mouth biters can't smell it."

Happy reached inside the case and took out a jar marked BURP. He peered inside. "Why is this one empty?"

"It won't be for long!" Karl said. "Wolfenstein always comes to the halftime show at the Muck Bowl. Teams who play in the bowl get to meet him. I can't wait. I'm going to ask him to burp into the jar . . . and then my collection will be complete!"

Happy grinned. "My uncle says you're only going

to make the Muck Bowl if I stay on the team and you don't lose every game. And even then, you'll get destroyed by the Frankensteins. They're so tough, they eat bricks like popcorn!"

Karl held up a paw. He didn't want to hear that. "As long as we win at least one of the next two games, we'll be invited. That's why we all need to pull together and really push forward!"

"'Push forward'?" Happy asked with glee. "You mean like *this*?" One of his tentacles shot out and pushed the vial containing the chunky foot fungus out of the case.

"No!" Karl shouted, and dove for the vial. Too late.

*Clink!* The vial hit the floor and shattered. The stench of the foot fungus instantly filled the fort.

"Wolfsbane!" Karl took a breath and tried to calm down. "That's okay, Happy," he said. "Accidents happen."

Happy giggled. "Oh, that wasn't an accident. And neither is this. Or this!" He knocked the jars with the sneeze and the armpit sweat out of the case. As they broke on the floor, Happy continued knocking loose the rest of the jars. Karl caught the last, but it was the empty one labeled BURP. All of the other vials in his most special collection had shattered!

"Hee hoo hee!" Happy laughed. "Got to go, but thanks for the party. I have a feeling the entertainment is about to arrive." Karl and his friends could hear him laughing "Hee hoo hee!" as he climbed down and left.

An instant later, rumbling filled the air.

"What's that?" Dennis wondered out loud.

Mike looked out the window and then back at them. "Uh-oh," he said. "Get ready for trouble."

# CHAPTER 6
## Herd of Mouth

Karl looked out the window, too. Using their tongues, a herd of nearly a hundred mini mouth biters was racing up the trunk of the tree.

"They're after the foot fungus!" Karl shouted.

They poured into Karl's tree fort and swarmed over the chunky foot fungus. In a flash, they gobbled it up. But the tiny, sharp-toothed monsters were still hungry.

They started chewing on everything in sight. Karl's posters. His chairs. The table.

The Scream Team huddled together as the

mouth biters started eating the floor. In seconds, the fort's walls and ceiling collapsed, crashing to the ground twenty feet below.

Dennis shrieked and flew straight up, getting tangled in the top branches of the pus-bag tree like a kite. Three of the biters had the edges of J.D.'s legs and were pinning him against the tree trunk. And a few were chewing along strips of Maxwell's wrapping like it was pasta.

The floor tilted and the rest of the monsters tumbled out. They all grabbed ahold of different branches, including Karl, who watched a table piled with football programs, old chin straps, and stitching from playoff-game footballs slide toward the edge of the fort.

As the table shot to the ground past him, Karl's paw was slipping on the branch. He was going to fall!

Just then, a pus bag sailed through the air. It struck the mouth biter on the ground under Karl.

*Splat!*

The stinky pus in the bag exploded on the monster's sharp teeth. Instantly the creature turned green, let out a "Blach!" and scurried out of the backyard.

"Mini mouth biters are allergic to pus!" Patsy yelled from her spot in the tree where she dangled over Karl. She was holding Eric between her ankles.

The bombs of pus bags kept raining down. Karl twisted around so he could see where they were coming from.

It was Beck!

The bigfoot was down on the ground and kicking the pus bags with sharpshooter accuracy. He'd pluck up a pus bag from near the tree and *smack!* He kicked with one foot and then the other, but always right on target.

One by one, Beck quickly drove away the mini biting monsters. In a few minutes, the backyard was clear and the Scream Team dropped from the tree. Eric bounced on the ground and started rolling in circles triumphantly around Beck.

"Beck, you did it!" Patsy said. "You saved the day!"

As the rest of the monsters gathered around him, Beck looked as if he might actually crack a smile. Something he hadn't done since Happy joined them.

"Why don't you kick like that on the football field, Beck?" Karl asked, slapping him on the back. "We'd win our next game against the Zombies for sure!"

Suddenly, Beck looked miserable again. "The team might win," he said, "but I'd lose. Everyone would laugh at my feet."

"Dude, you're a *big*foot," J.D. said. "Isn't that kind of who you are?"

"Sure, I guess." Beck nodded. "I just don't want to be the *biggest* foot."

He shuffled off, heading out the gate.

For a second, Karl thought he could still hear the echo of Happy's laughter. "Hee hoo hee!"

# CHAPTER 7
## Save that Pigskin!

All that week, Karl tried to talk to the Coaches Conundrum about Happy. But the Scream Team couldn't get rid of him without forfeiting the season and giving up an invite to the Muck Bowl. Besides, Virgil and Wyatt were still too busy arguing about offense versus defense to deal with any other problems.

The night of the game against the Zombies, the coaches were on the sidelines but seemed to be on another planet. They were both wearing new headsets

and yelling into the microphones attached to them.

"In this new play, we'll score for sure!" Wyatt shouted, sounding offensive.

"No!" Virgil cried defensively. "If anything, with this new play we'll get rid of the chance that we won't score."

As the coaches bickered before kickoff, spectators kept pouring into the stands. Monsters were coming from all over to see the game.

"I'm not surprised," Maxwell said. "I have quite a large fan club."

But Karl knew the fans were there to watch a different player on the Scream Team . . . Happy. Everyone had heard about Happy's tricks and wanted to see what pranks he would pull next.

And they didn't have to wait long. When Hester the Zombie kicked the ball to start the game, Patsy waved her arm to signal a fair catch.

"Fair catch?" Happy shouted to the crowd. "Does she want to catch a fair?" Happy pulled out a toy merry-go-round and a mini roller coaster from under his uniform. He threw them at Patsy. "There's your fair!" he cried.

Patsy got so confused, she caught the toys but not the football, which bounced off her head and rolled down the field. The Zombies recovered the ball at the 15-yard line, and the fans went crazy. As they cackled and cheered, Karl could see Happy's grin get bigger and he took a little bow.

"What a ham!" J.D. scoffed. "He's totally lapping up the attention!"

For the rest of the game, Happy ran offsides on purpose, tripped his teammates, and dipped their mouth guards in tongue-shrinking juice. All his pranks allowed the Zombies to easily beat the Scream Team by four touchdowns. The excited fans started chanting Happy's name.

Karl could feel his dream of going to the Muck Bowl slipping away.

At their next game, against the Swine Creatures, the stands were even more packed with monsters. A dragon held up a poster that said HAPPY TO SEE YOU! and a three-headed dog waved a sign that read HEE! HOO! HEE!

Happy focused almost completely on getting the crowd to cheer for him. When they seemed a little bored by his same old tricks, Happy had to dream up new elaborate schemes. He made up a tap dance he called "Do the Happy!" Soon all the fans were following his lead and stomping in their seats.

Lucky for the Scream Team, the Swine Creatures had their own problems. Whenever someone threw the ball or kicked it, the Swine players would panic and oink. "No!" they would squeal. "Call for help! Don't let it fall!"

"What's up with them?" Mike asked as two Swines grabbed the football and ran off the field.

"They *are* Swine Creatures," J.D. said, "and the football *is* called a pigskin."

"Now you're just making me hungry," Dennis said, drooling.

With Happy distracted by the crowd and the Swine Creatures afraid to hurt the ball, the Scream Team managed to pull off the Statue of Bitterly play.

Karl pretended to hand off the ball to Beck, and then threw it to Patsy. His pass was wild, but J.D. caught it. He spun, raced down the field, and scored a touchdown.

With a score of 7 to 0, the Scream Team had defeated the Swine Creatures!

"We actually won!" Patsy said after the game. "And we didn't kick Happy off. You know what that means?"

"We're going to the Wolfenstein Muck Bowl!" Mike cried.

Eric bounced up and down and the team cheered. But not Karl. He wasn't celebrating.

"What's wrong, Karl?" J.D. asked. "Isn't this what you wanted?"

It was. Except, now he had a new worry.

Karl and his teammates had gone through so much to be considered a real team. Now, thanks to Happy, they were the league's biggest joke.

Would they look like fools in front of his all-time hero, Wolfenstein? Would he start laughing at them, too?

# CHAPTER 8
## Bowled Over

Four days later, the night of the Wolfenstein Muck Bowl finally arrived!

Karl woke up feeling queasy and anxious, but he knew he couldn't miss this game. Even if things went horribly wrong, at least Karl would finally meet his hero Wolfenstein at halftime.

That would make up for all of Happy's mean pranks.

When he arrived at the stadium on his bike, the Scream Team, Mr. Benedict, and the Coaches

Conundrum were already there. The coaches were both wearing their headsets and yelling into them. They didn't seem to notice anyone around them.

While the rest of the Scream Team stretched before the game, Happy warmed up the crowd by imitating his teammates. He rolled into the goalpost like he was Eric and chased an invisible tail as if he were Karl. But the crowd especially loved it when he imitated Beck.

"Squish, squish." Happy made sound effects and stomped around in the muck. "Look at me, everybody, I'm Beck the flipper foot! Abso-tootly!"

The crowd roared with laughter. Karl was just about to imitate a werewolf biting someone when Hairy Hairwell's voice blasted over the speakers.

"What a night for football here in Putridge Stadium!" he shouted. "The air at the annual Wolfenstein Muck Bowl is crackling with excitement as we await the arrival of All-Time All-Star Wolfenstein at the halftime show!"

The spectators whooped and cheered.

"And of course, on either side of the halftime show, we have some football for you," Hairy said with a chuckle. "We have a mismatched matchup tonight. Say hello to the usually dogged underdogs, the Scream Team. . . ."

Hairy paused so the Scream Team could wave to the crowd. Karl thought he could hear someone clapping. Then he realized it was just the sound of Dennis's wings flapping nervously together.

"And," Hairy continued, "please give a warm welcome to the unstoppable Frankenstein's Monsters!"

The crowd went wild. Turning toward the other team's bench, Karl got his first good look at the Frankensteins. "Wolfsbane," he said. Now he could guess why they didn't let Bolt on their team.

Bolt had a leg that belonged to a ballet dancer, one arm from a teacher's pet, the other arm from a gardener, and a mishmash of different parts.

Not the monsters on the Frankensteins.

Their linemen had legs the size of tree trunks, from sumo wrestlers. Their running back, Josie, had springy feet from a high jumper. The Frankenstein wide receiver, Hayden, had hands like tennis rackets, from a worker who had gotten stuck under a steamroller. And all of their players were at least twice as tall as Bolt.

When Frank the Cyclops called for the coin toss, the Frankenstein quarterback, Leo, thudded out to the 50-yard line like a moving block of granite. He cast a shadow like a skyscraper over Karl.

"Leo hungry," Leo grunted. Karl just hoped werewolf wasn't on the menu.

The ref flipped the coin. The Frankensteins won the coin toss and elected to kick. Both teams' players lined up to start the game.

"Uh-oh," Mike said nervously. Karl couldn't blame him. The Scream Team looked like tiny squish-ants compared to the giant-sized Frankensteins.

"Just make it until halftime," Karl told himself. "And it will all be worth it."

Lillian the Frankenstein kicked the ball long and high.

As the wave of humungous Frankensteins lumbered toward him, Karl wasn't sure he would even make it past this play.

# CHAPTER 9
## Oh Gnome You Didn't

The rest of the Scream Team scattered, leaving Karl to catch the ball. He snagged it out of the air and started running down the field.

That was when a tiny voice started speaking in his head. "This is so scary and totally not worth it," the voice said. "You should just turn around and run home."

For a second, Karl thought about following that advice when—*Wham!*

Edward the Frankenstein slammed into him.

"Fumble!" Hairy shouted as the ball flew out of Karl's paws. Edward caught it but tripped before he could gain any ground.

Meanwhile, Karl was still flying high up into the air and had a good view of the field.

All the monsters on the Scream Team were acting strangely. Eric was rolling in circles, Bolt was digging a hole, and Dennis was gnawing on the bottom of the goalpost as if it were made of headcheese.

Karl splashed into the muck helmet-first. "What are you guys doing?" he asked his teammates as he got back on his feet. And why did one side of his shoulder pads feel kind of squirmy? Karl jabbed it with his paw, and the pad said, "Ouch!"

A grizzled little head popped through his uniform where his shoulder pad should have been.

"It's a gnome-it-all!" Karl yelled. The mini monsters were famous for giving incredibly bad advice. Soon the heads were pushing through the uniform fabric of all the members of the Scream Team . . . except for Happy.

"The Scream Team seems to be having an equipment malfunction," Hairy announced. "It seems someone has swapped gnomes in place of their shoulder pads. But who would do something so wicked?"

"I did it!" Happy shouted to the crowd. "Hee hoo hee!"

"Hee hoo hee!" the spectators cheered back.

"Now I know how the Conundrums feel," Patsy said, giving the gnome on her shoulder a little flick.

After a turnover of downs and fixing their shoulder pads, the team hurried back out onto the field to play defense. "We've got to hold them!" Karl called from his position at corner back.

But now the Scream Team was too worried about Happy to concentrate. What would he do next?

Tommy, the Frankenstein center, snapped the ball to Leo. The offensive line tore through the Scream Team's defense.

With all the time in the world, Leo stepped back and nailed the pass to his wide receiver, Hayden, who rolled down the field like a tank.

Hairy Hairwell kept up with the play-by-play: "Hayden's at the 25 and 20. . . . No Scream Team players are even close. . . . He's at 15, 10, 5 . . . touchdown! This is a doomsday scenario for the Scream Team!"

The Frankensteins went for a two-point conversion and easily picked it up, then kicked the ball to the Scream Team. As the football headed straight for him, Mike the swamp thing turned even more green. He waved his hands frantically—and then his tail just to be safe—to signal a fair catch.

On the first play, Karl took the snap from Patsy. He went for the pitch back to Beck, and Beck broke to the right. A clear path to the end zone was open in front of him. He started running.

"The Frankensteins didn't see that play coming!" Hairy announced. "Beck could actually go all the way!"

"Yeah, right," Happy yelled so monsters in the stands could hear him. "On those spatulas? I don't think so."

The laughter from the crowd was like an invisible force field. It stopped Beck in his tracks. But he didn't stay still for long.

*Kablam!* Kevin, the Frankenstein middle linebacker, slammed into him like a freight train, sending him back ten yards and dropping him at the 45-yard line.

That was when Happy called a time-out.

"What are you doing?" Karl demanded. "Beck actually gained some ground. We're on a roll!"

Happy started laughing so hard, he had to lie down in the muck. "You're all like my crunch bug puppets in my show! I am the puppet master!"

The rest of the first two quarters of the game was a blur of Happy pranks, Scream Team missteps, and Frankenstein tackles. Karl kept waving to get the Conundrums' attention, but they were still shouting into the headsets and paying no mind.

Then a cannon went off with a loud *bang*.

"What was that?" Dennis asked in shock. All eyes went to Happy as if he were behind the explosion. He grinned.

"Wasn't me." Happy laughed. Frank the ref had fired the cannon. Karl realized it was halftime.

It was time to meet Wolfenstein!

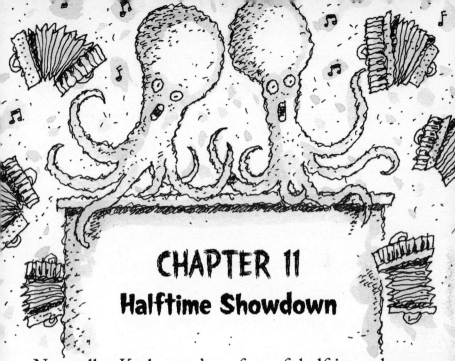

# CHAPTER 11
## Halftime Showdown

Normally, Karl wasn't a fan of halftime shows. A year ago at the Wolfenstein Bowl, The Squid Screechers screamed the song "I Ink I Love You" while eating a truckful of accordions. And another year, the Blobs did an aerial dramatic reenactment of Paint Drying on Pond Scum.

But nothing would keep Karl from being part of this halftime show. Not even the fact that they were losing the game 8 to 0.

*This is it!* he thought, clutching the empty BURP

jar in one paw. *I will finally get to meet Wolfenstein!* Moments before Wolfenstein was set to arrive, the Scream Team gathered with the Frankensteins on either side of the 50-yard line. The fog machine clicked on and the laser lights spun. Dr. Neuron came down from his skybox and stood at the podium at center field.

"Ladies and gentlemen," Dr. Neuron said into the microphone. "It is my great honor as JCML president to introduce you to the one . . . the only . . . Wolfenstein!"

Dr. Neuron pointed to the ramp leading to the locker rooms as the band started playing "Wail to the Grief." All of the crowd's eyes, tentacles, and feelers turned to look at the ramp.

"Here he comes!" someone screamed in the stands.

But instead of Wolfenstein, it was a small snail creature. He emerged from the fog, carrying a paper bag and leaving behind a trail of goo.

"That must be his bodyguard," Mike whispered to Patsy.

"Shhh," Karl said. He didn't want to miss a single second!

Everyone watched as the snail creature inched its way to the podium. It reached its slimy head into the paper bag, grabbed a note with its mouth, and handed it to Dr. Neuron.

Then, with all eyes still on it, the snail began the slow, slimy trip back to the gate, where it disappeared into the fog.

Dr. Neuron opened the note and read it. His tentacles drooped, and he whispered something, then more loudly he said, "Wolfenstein isn't coming!"

The band screeched to a halt. There were gasps, gulps, and shrieks from the stands.

"Someone sent Wolfenstein a message," Dr. Neuron said. "It told him that the Muck Bowl had been moved to the middle of the ocean. He's on a freighter right now heading out to sea."

Monsters started weeping. Even Frank the Cyclops had what looked like a puddle-sized tear pooling in his one giant eye.

"Who would trick Wolfenstein like this?" Dr. Neuron asked as he gazed up into the stands. "Who? I ask you . . . who?"

The monsters looked at each other's faces, trying to find the culprit. That was when Happy shouted, "Me! It was me!"

Dr. Neuron's eyes bugged out a little. Now everyone was staring at Happy. He jumped up and down on the field next to the Scream Team. He seemed to love the attention. "I did it!" he yelled. "I sent the note!"

"Uh . . . ," Dr. Neuron said, as if he had no idea what to say. "I have an urgent meeting to attend."

Dr. Neuron hurried away from the podium, hopped into his nearby limo, and was gone in a squeal of tires. He had faced angry crowds before and knew it was time to get out of there.

Karl's fur stood straight up and he stormed over to Happy. "You!" The werewolf jabbed a paw toward Happy. "Look what you've done!"

Happy started to laugh. "Hee hoo—!"

Karl interrupted him. "You knew how important meeting Wolfenstein was to me. I want you off the Scream Team."

"You can't always get what you want. You absotootly can't play without me. You'd have to forfeit. It's in the rules." Happy started giggling and turned to the audience. "Did you hear what this shaved cat just said?" he yelled to them. "Isn't that *purr*-fect, everyone?"

But no one else laughed. The crowd just silently stared at Happy, clearly angry about Wolfenstein not showing.

"Hee hoo hee?" Happy said. But no one responded. His smile cracked. Without the audience cheering him on, he seemed to deflate and his tentacles drooped.

"You don't even want to be on the Scream Team!" Patsy said. "Why don't you just quit, Happy?"

"If I quit, I won't get my crunch bug puppet theater, and . . ." Happy's voice trailed off like maybe that wasn't the most important thing anymore. "You love football, Karl. And you'd give it all up just to get me off the team?"

Karl didn't say anything, he just looked at the empty BURP jar in his hand. Workers had cleared away the podium and were cleaning up the rest of the field. Halftime was almost over.

Happy looked at the jar and stepped closer to Karl. "If you let me destroy the Scream Team now, people will always laugh at you. You and your friends will be a joke forever. And believe me, I know about jokes."

"*Bad* jokes," Karl snarled.

"But," Happy said, "if you keep playing, I'll be a real part of the team. I'll stop trying to destroy you."

Frank the Cyclops blew his whistle. The second half was about to start.

Karl had to make a decision. Could he trust Happy? Or was this just one more big joke?

# CHAPTER 12
## A Real Head for Football

"Welcome back to the Wolfenstein Muck Bowl!" Harry Hairwell called from the announcer's booth. "I'm surprised to see that the Scream Team hasn't fled the stadium! After that disastrous first half, odds are they're about to be crushed by the Frankensteins."

"He's right," Karl said as the team gathered near their bench. "We need to score eight points against the toughest team in the league just to tie things up."

"Does that mean the Scream Team is still together?" J.D. asked hopefully. "And that we're playing the second half?"

Karl smiled and nodded. The Scream Team cheered.

Holding up a paw, Karl said, "But only if Happy promises to really help out the team."

"Abso-tootly," Happy said. "Let me start here." He walked over to the Conundrums and pulled off their headsets.

"What are you doing?" Coach Wyatt demanded.

"The headsets I gave you are only connected to each other," Happy explained.

Virgil rubbed his ears and looked at Wyatt. "You mean I've been talking to you this whole time?"

"You're the one who put me on hold for twenty minutes?" Wyatt snapped.

As the Conundrums started bickering again, Karl led the Scream Team out to the field to kick the ball.

"Come on, Beck," Karl said. "We need you to

kick. Things are different now. Happy won't make fun of you anymore."

Beck shook his head. "That hasn't changed the size of my feet. Or the fact that all the monsters in the stands will still laugh at me."

In the end, Eric the blob tried kicking but it was more like a bounce. The ball rolled right into the hands of Ali of the Frankensteins. She lumbered down the field slowly. Karl could guess why. She probably thought Happy would keep messing up his own team and that she had all the time in the world.

Out of nowhere, a blur of tentacles tangled itself around her legs. Ali tripped and came crashing down into the muck.

Karl couldn't believe it. Happy had just tackled the Frankenstein!

"That's what I'm talking about," Happy said, getting to his feet. "Hee hoo hee!"

Now that the Frankensteins didn't have Happy's help, it wasn't as easy for them to get a first down. They went three and out, and kicked to the Scream Team.

Karl tried calling running and passing plays, but the Frankensteins' defense kept driving the Scream Team back. Soon it was fourth and 45 on their own 5-yard line.

Patsy snapped the ball to Karl. He tossed it to Beck in the backfield.

"Punt!" Karl shouted.

Beck hesitated and stumbled backward. Now he was in the Scream Team's end zone with the ball.

"Beck of the Scream Team has two choices," Hairy announced. "He can't run the ball through that wall of Frankensteins. He can punt the ball or get tackled. That would put the Scream Team down by two more points and the game would definitely be over for them."

Beck paused for one more second. Then he dropped the ball. As if trying to hide his foot, he waited until just before the ball hit the ground, then brought his leg up and punted.

Even at a fraction of the power, the punt rocketed through the air. But way to the right. It shot over the stands and into the parking lot. For a moment, the crowd was stunned.

"Wow, that's some foot on that bigfoot!" Hairy yelled. Karl could tell he wasn't trying to be mean, but it was the worst thing he could say. The spectators started laughing and Beck hung his head.

"That's okay, Beck," Happy said. When Beck flinched, waiting for a cruel punch line, Happy added, "Abso-tootly okay."

The Frankensteins took the ball at the Scream Team's 20. Leo stepped back to make a short pass. Before he could throw the ball, Happy called out, "Look over there! It's angry villagers with pitchforks!"

Distracted, Leo threw the ball too low and Bolt intercepted it. The Scream Team had possession!

"We don't fight dirty, Happy," Karl said, shaking his head.

"Okay, okay," Happy said. "Just think of all the ways I messed us up in the first half. That just evened things out a little."

The clock continued to tick down, but the Scream Team couldn't seem to move the ball down the field. At the end of each play, Patsy kept exploding like a party favor. No matter how the play went and even if no one was near her, pieces of her body flew here and there.

"Keep it together, Patsy," Karl told her when they were in the huddle. "It's fourth and 20. We all need to keep our heads."

"Maybe not," Happy said. "This could actually be the perfect time to lose a head or two."

Karl thought for a second. "Good point, Happy," he said, and then called the play. "Zombie Sneak on two."

The Scream Team lined up, and Karl shouted, "Hut one! Hut two!"

Patsy performed the snap, and something flew past Karl and rolled onto the field.

"The snap has gone bad!" Hairy Hairwell shouted. "The ball is loose! Fumble!"

The Frankensteins fell on the ball like a mob of anvils. Each monster grabbed for it. Finally, Ali the Frankenstein pulled free and held up a round object.

"Looks like the Frankensteins have recovered the ball!" Hairy announced. "Hold on . . . is that ball smiling?"

It was. Because it wasn't the football.

Ali realized it at the same time. "Not ball!" she yelled. "Not ball!"

She was holding Patsy's head. "Hello, Ali," Patsy said with a grin. "How you doing today?"

Meanwhile Patsy's body was running down the field. She had replaced her head with the football. As she stepped into the end zone and the play ended, Patsy exploded into pieces.

"Touchdown!" Hairy yelled. "The Scream Team has scored a touchdown!"

The crowd didn't seem to know how to react. They were used to laughing at the Scream Team, not cheering.

"I don't get the joke," a squid creature said.

Back in the huddle, Karl gave Patsy a high five . . . and then her head back. She screwed it back on but seemed a little dizzy. "Whoa, I'm seeing triple!" she said. "Maybe Happy should go back to being center, at least for the next play."

Karl wasn't sure. With only seconds on the clock, the next play could be their *last* play. The Scream Team had six points on the board but needed the two-point conversion to tie things up.

"Let me do this for the Scream Team, Karl," Happy said. "I won't turn it into a joke."

Finally, Karl nodded. Everyone deserved a second chance.

The Frankensteins relaxed when they saw Happy back at center. They seemed to think he was back to

his usual self and this was part of one of his pranks. Karl hoped they weren't right.

*Only one way to find out*, he thought.

Karl called, "Hut one! Hut two!" and this time, Happy snapped the ball perfectly. It wedged right between Karl's paws with a satisfying *smack!* Karl took advantage of the Frankensteins' surprise to run the ball across the line and score two points.

"I can't believe it!" Hairy shouted. "Never in the history of football has anyone seen a game like this. It's all tied up. Fiends and ghouls, we're going into overtime!"

# CHAPTER 13
## Sudden-Life Overtime

"We're in sudden death!" Hairy shouted.

"It's not so sudden for me," Patsy said. "I've been undead for years."

"The first team to score will win the Wolfenstein Muck Bowl," Hairy continued. "And have the bragging rights for the next year!"

To decide who would kick and receive, George called Karl and Leo out to the 50-yard line for another coin toss. This time Karl won, and he instantly said, "The Scream Team will receive."

Karl knew that the minute they gave up possession of the football, they would lose. The Scream Team had been lucky so far, but once the Frankensteins had the ball, they'd just stomp all the way down the field.

The Frankenstein kick landed straight in J.D.'s hands. He made it five yards to the Scream Team's 45 before being tackled by an avalanche of Frankensteins.

Karl was determined to lead his team. He took the snap and then stepped away to make a pass. It wobbled toward Eric. A Frankenstein swatted the pass out of the air . . . and then Karl's next pass, too. The Frankensteins' defense would not let up. One more broken play and it was fourth and 15. Karl used their one and only sudden-death time-out.

The team gathered on the sidelines next to the Coaches Conundrum.

"Well, that was fun while it lasted," Mike said with a disappointed shrug.

"It's not over yet," Karl said. "We're going for the

field goal. We could score first and win the game."

"No way!" J.D. said. "That'd be an 85-yard kick, something no one in the JCML has ever done. And we don't even have a kicker!"

"Yes," Wyatt said, and Virgil added, "We do."

"Where?" Dennis asked, as if worried the coaches meant him.

"It's you, Beck," the Coaches Conundrum answered at the same time.

Beck shook his head. "The whole crowd will just laugh at me."

Karl started to say something, but Happy stepped forward first. "No," he said. "They'll be laughing at me."

In a flash, Happy darted closer to the stands. He slipped off his shoes, put them on his ears, and started trying to walk through the muck on his face. The spectators started giggling immediately.

"Who's Happy making fun of now?" Beck groaned.

"Himself," Karl answered. It was true. For once, Happy was the punch line of one of his own jokes.

Beck watched the crowd point and laugh at Happy. Finally, he called, "Hey, Happy! You can knock it off!"

Happy flipped upright and hurried back to the bench. "See, Beck?" he said. "I didn't melt from them laughing at me. Who cares what other monsters think?"

"I do," Beck said.

"Wait—" Happy started to say.

"No, it's okay," Beck said. "I want the crowd to look at my feet. I want other monsters to see what I can do with them."

And then, for the first time in weeks, he smiled. "I want to kick the ball."

The Scream Team cheered.

"Monstrous!" Coach Virgil shouted. "Now get back out there!"

The Frankensteins were already on the field, making grumbling sounds like they couldn't wait to start tackling smaller monsters again. Karl and his teammates rushed into formation. Karl would take the snap on *three* from Happy and hold the ball for Beck.

"Hee hoo hee." Happy laughed. Karl shot him a look, and Happy slapped his tentacles over his mouth. "Sorry! I laugh when I get nervous, or when someone is trying for an 85-yard field goal."

Karl gave Beck one more smile. "You can do it, Beck." Then he got ready to call for the snap.

"The Scream Team is going for a record today . . . the longest field goal in JCML history," Hairy

Hairwell announced as he described the action. "Here's the snap. And Beck the bigfoot comes in for the kick. It's over the Frankensteins' arms. The kick is high and it's going long. Fiends and ghouls, this ball is soaring . . . it's on target for the goalposts. . . ."

Hairy had to take a breath, before yelling, "The kick is . . . good! It's GOOD! The Scream Team hits it in sudden death. The game is over! The game IS over! The Scream Team wins the game!"

# CHAPTER 14
## Whatever Makes You Happy

The Scream Team went berserk. "You did it, Beck!" Karl shouted.

But Beck wasn't listening. He was too busy kicking anything that wasn't nailed down. His helmet. Patsy's elbow. The cooler that was empty after the team dumped the hot slime on the Coaches Conundrum.

Beck had rediscovered something amazing. His own talent. He kept kicking . . . and kicking! Objects soared through the air like confetti at a ticker-tape parade.

"Monstrous job, Scream Team!" Coach Virgil cheered.

"All right," Coach Wyatt said. "Let's tell the Frankensteins how well they played today."

They went through the handshake line with the Frankensteins. Leo accidentally gave Karl a high five that nearly knocked his paw off, but said, "Game good."

And then, like they always did after a good game, the Scream Team jumped into a huge team pileup. The Coaches Conundrum hopped in and so did Mr. Benedict. They were all laughing.

Except one monster.

Karl saw that Happy wasn't smiling or grinning or giggling or chuckling or laughing. Standing off on his own, he just looked kind of sad.

Karl trotted over to him. "You did good out there."

"Yeah," Happy said. "Doesn't feel like the crowd thought that."

When Beck had scored the field goal, the crowd hadn't really cheered. They had come to see Happy make fun of people, and seemed disappointed when it turned out to be just a regular football game.

"Welcome to the Scream Team!" Karl said. "They'll know how good we are someday and we'll get the respect we deserve." Karl had a thought. He grabbed his empty glass jar from the sidelines.

"What are you doing with that?" Happy asked.

Karl scraped the word BURP off the jar. He opened it, waved it around in the air, and then sealed it back up.

"Is that for your collection?" Happy said, then looked ashamed. "The one I destroyed?"

"No, it's for you," Karl said. "It's called the smell of victory and teamwork."

"Thanks," Happy said quietly, putting the jar in his pocket. He shook his head. "Because of those two games I made the Scream Team lose, it will never make it to the championship game. Not that I'll be playing in more games, anyway. I guess you'll boot me off the team now and find someone else for my spot."

Happy started shuffling away as Patsy and J.D. came over to stand next to Karl. "Is there a gnome-it-all on my shoulder?" Karl asked them.

"Why?" J.D. asked.

"Because I'm about to do something that might be kind of a bad idea," Karl said, and then he shouted, "Hey, Happy! You want to stay on the team?"

Happy stopped but didn't turn around. "Not without the magic word." Then he turned to face them. "*Sorry* is the magic word, and I have to say it." He took a breath. "I'm really sorry for everything I did."

Karl could tell Happy meant it.

"So are you going to stay?" Patsy asked.

"Maybe just until the end of football season." Happy looked at her. "Would that make all of you happy?"

"I hope not!" Karl said, grinning. "Can you imagine a team of Happys?"

"See?" Happy laughed. "You really are a funny cat when you want to be!"

# Scream Team

**BECK THE BIGFOOT**

**Number:** 21  *that's my shoe size!*

**Position:** Kicker  *or punter*

**Favorite Play:** Anything by playwright Horton Foote  *No! It's the kickoff*

**Football Hero:** Twinkle Toes Malone
*He plays with a lot of sole!*

**Best Instrument:** Tuba
*Actually, it's the shoehorn*

**Hobby:** Blushing
*Not anymore . . . I'm proud of my flipper-sized feet!*

**Favorite saying:** "I put my foot in my mouth!"
*I do that all day!*

**Future Goal:** Dip toes in two oceans
*At the same time (only kidding!)*

**Place to Improve:** Smelly feet
*They do not!*

**Nickname:** Biggest Foot

*How about just Beck?*

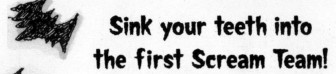